PRIDE
of the
Prairie

WRITTEN BY RENAE SCOTT
Illustrated by Rachel Brixius

ISBN: 1453722645
ISBN-13: 9781453722640

For our son,
you fill our hearts with pride.

Welcome to the land of ice and snow
where basketball players seldom go.

Our story is about a special team,
who worked hard together
to live out their dreams.

With nothing to lose and glory to gain.
Their drive and determination
were hard to contain.

They came to Fargo as boys and left town as men.

You still hear their names now and again.

To **NDSU** they brought
much pride and glory.

It sounds like a fable,
but this is their true story.

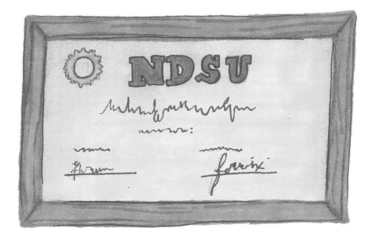

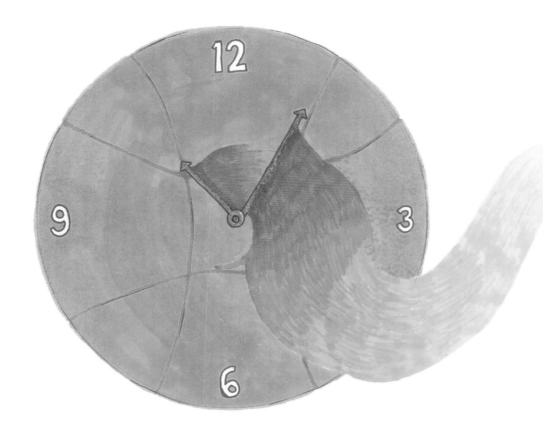

We're getting ahead of ourselves.
Let's go back to the start.

It was one team's success,
but many people played a part.

The Bison once played at the level called division two.
The president said, "This isn't right for grand old SU."

Soon he announced,
"We're going to division one,

Bring on the competition it will be a lot of fun."

They said, "It was crazy.
The Bison couldn't compete."

With no time to be lazy, the coaches began to search for that Division one athlete.

The core of the team came from our region.

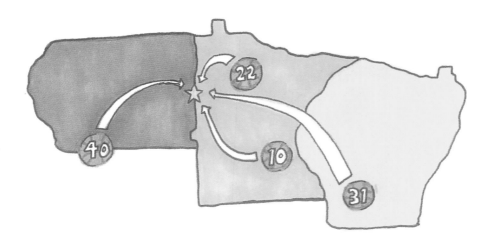

Four years given up to play in one game
in one special season.

For five long years
the team practiced and trained.

No chance of post season
and not one complained.

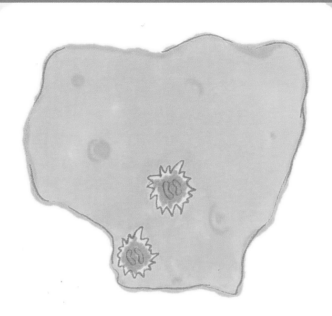

The Bison quickly showed they could compete with the best.

Big wins over Marquette and Wisconsin
earned Coach Miles a new job out west.

Coach Phillips moved up and took over the reigns.

The messenger was different but the message had not changed.

Change isn't easy, but it must have been fate. He proclaimed, "In 2009 it will happen, tell the fans to save the date."

9   Summit League 10
    Tournament
      2009

    NDSU vs. Oakland

That season was filled with more ups than downs.
Regular season champs the Bison were crowned.

Regular Season Champions

The team had earned the tournament's top seed.
Opportunity was there, but nothing guaranteed.

The team traveled south in search of their prize.

No sign of fear,
just fire in their eyes.

A late winter blizzard
closed the road to the fans.

But when the game
started, green and yellow
filled the stands.

At first they were down
but weathered the storm.

They came thundering back
in true Bison form.

Five years of hard work
came down to just three games.

When the last buzzer, sounded
the whole nation knew their names.

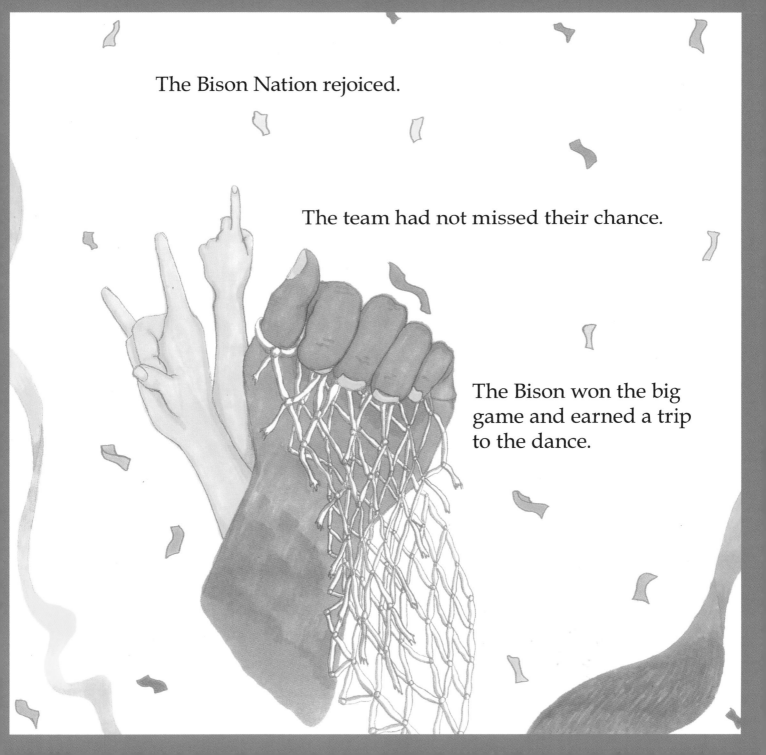

The Bison Nation rejoiced.

The team had not missed their chance.

The Bison won the big game and earned a trip to the dance.

The first round of the dance did not go their way.

Try as they might, it just wasn't their day.

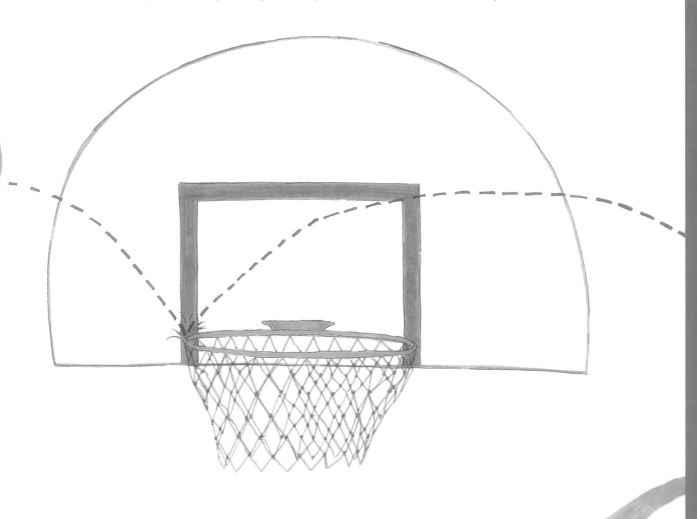

The Bison walked off the court with heads held up high;
for the Bison had filled the prairie with pride.

GO BISON!

Autographs

8432662R2

Made in the USA
Charleston, SC
09 June 2011